My Mother Talks to Trees

To those who plant and protect trees.

—*D. G.*

To Allen B., for his unfailing support and encouragement.

—*M. M.*

Published by
PEACHTREE PUBLISHERS
1700 Chattahoochee Avenue
Atlanta, Georgia 30318-2112
www.peachtree-online.com

Text © 1999 by Doris Gove
Jacket and interior color illustrations © 1999 by Marilynn H. Mallory
Glossary line art illustrations © 1999 by Vicky Holifield

First trade paperback edition published 2005

Jacket and book design by Loraine M. Balcsik and Marilynn H. Mallory
Glossary and line drawings by Vicky Holifield

Manufactured in China

10 9 8 7 6 5 4 3 (hardcover edition)
10 9 8 7 6 5 4 3 2 1 (trade paperback edition)

Library of Congress Cataloging-in-Publication Data

Gove, Doris.
    My mother talks to trees / Doris Gove; illustrated by Marilynn H.
Mallory. —1st ed.
        p. cm.
    Summary: Although embarrassed when her mother stops and
talks to all the trees on their walk, a girl joins her in admiring their
leaves, flowers, needles, and seeds and recognizes them as a source
of beauty.
    ISBN 1-56145-166-5 (hardcover)
    ISBN 1-56145-336-6 (paperback)
    [1. Trees—Fiction.] I. Mallory, Marilynn H., ill. II. Title.
PZ7.G744My 1999
[Fic]—dc21   98-36188
                                                                 CIP
                                                                 AC

My Mother
Talks to Trees

Doris Gove

**Illustrated by
Marilynn H. Mallory**

PEACHTREE
ATLANTA

My mother
talks to trees.
Out loud and
right in public.

Like today, when we are walking home from school. It's spring, and all the trees have new baby leaves.

"Wow, little dogwood," she says, walking all the way around a small tree near the slide. "You're blooming this year. Congratulations! Six white flowers is great for the first time."

Mom shows me one of the flowers. It's pretty. Each white petal looks like it has a tiny bite taken out of it.

Then we walk down by the library.

"Redbud, you are beautiful," she says. "You came through that last snowstorm really well." When I see my friend Dana and her dad coming up to the library, I stand really close to the tree so they will think Mom is talking to me.

I notice that the redbud tree has flowers coming right out of the bark. Really weird! And they're not red, either. They're pink. The leaves look like green hearts.

Thank goodness there's nobody around on the next block, because Mom jumps up and catches a branch of a tall tree. She pulls it down so I can look at some fuzzy little caterpillars dangling from a twig. But they're not caterpillars.

"Hickory, look at your catkins!" she exclaims. "These boy flowers of yours will be dropping pollen in just a few days."

"Where are the girl flowers?" I ask.

"They're on higher branches, and they will grow into hickory nuts," she explains. We count the leaflets on each leaf stem. There are two or three on each side and one on the end.

Down the street, she shakes hands with my friend Jonathan's Christmas tree. His dad planted it in their yard after Christmas last year. "Hello, blue spruce," says Mom. "You've got lots of good new growth—you're going to get big this year." A car goes by and the people stare.

The old needles are bluish green and sharp on the end. I break off a little sprig to smell the Christmas smell. The light green new needles are soft. Mom says the tree came from Colorado, but it can grow here.

Around the corner, we stop at a tree with leaves that look like mittens. "Oh, you poor sassafras," Mom says. "I'll get some of that honeysuckle vine off your branches. There, you can stretch out easier now."

I take a closer look. Some of those sassafras leaves have three fingers, and some have *no* fingers at all!

I wonder if I should remind Mom that this isn't our yard.

She goes up to a big tree in the next yard and pats it. A dog barks at us from the porch.

"Hello, white oak!" she says. "I love your lichens." Her fingers trace the green crinkly circles that grow on the bark.

The leaves look like pieces from a giant jigsaw puzzle. Some old acorns crunch under my feet. I pick up an acorn hat and put it on the tip of my finger.

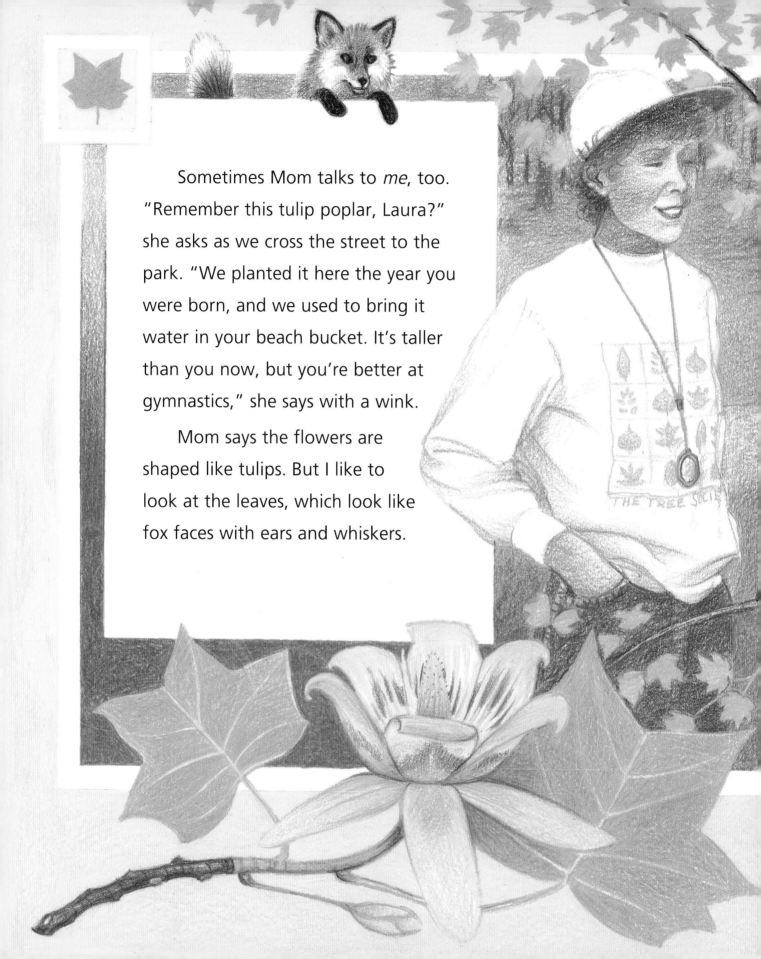

Sometimes Mom talks to *me*, too. "Remember this tulip poplar, Laura?" she asks as we cross the street to the park. "We planted it here the year you were born, and we used to bring it water in your beach bucket. It's taller than you now, but you're better at gymnastics," she says with a wink.

Mom says the flowers are shaped like tulips. But I like to look at the leaves, which look like fox faces with ears and whiskers.

"And you're growing fast, too," she says to a pine tree down the hill. "White pine," she tells me. "It's the only pine with five needles in each bunch—one needle for each letter in the word *white*."

She pulls a branch toward me. At the end are some things that look like Rice Krispies. She taps them and yellow powder floats out. "Laura, these are the male cones, or pollen makers. Conifers have cones instead of flowers and needles instead of leaves."

"They stay green all year, too," I say.

She pulls down a higher branch to show me the green female cone. We both get sticky pitch on our hands. On the very top branches are some big pine cones from last year.

"Hey maple, your seeds are almost ripe!" Mom shouts up into a tree that from a distance looks like a huge, bright green lollipop, like the trees I used to draw in kindergarten. Its wide leaves are bigger than my hand, and almost the same shape, too.

She picks a few seeds and we throw them up in the air. They spin on their helicopter wings. Mine go farther than Mom's.

Down the path in the park, we visit four little walnut trees. Three are as tall as I am, and the fourth comes up to my waist. Mom and I planted them on Arbor Day last year, and I carried milk jugs of water for the new trees. They just looked like sticks then, but now each one has a little umbrella of leaves.

"You all outdid yourselves," says Mom. "What graceful long leaves. I hope you like your new home." Then she adds, "In just a few years we'll be able to gather your delicious nuts."

Mom shows me how each leaf stem has one leaflet on the end and six or seven on each side. *Hey,* the walnut leaves are almost like the hickory leaves, but the walnut has more leaflets. The leaves smell spicy when I rub them between my fingers.

Mom calls out, "Hey, persimmon!" and heads toward a tall, straight tree with lichens on its bark. The persimmon tree bark looks as if it is made of little blocks. The shiny, dark leaves are pointy on both ends.

Mom pats the tree and says, "Thank you for the sweet persimmon fruits you gave us last fall." I hope my friend Whitney is not looking out her window from across the street.

As we walk toward the street, I look back at the new walnut trees. The bigger ones are standing tall and strong, but the small one is drooping a little. I run back and stroke one of its new leaves. It feels soft like velvet and smells great.

"Don't worry," I say. "We'll be back."

Getting to Know the Trees
in Your Neighborhood

Some words you need to know when you talk to trees:

 **Deciduous tree**—a tree that drops its leaves in the fall and grows new ones in the spring

 **Evergreen tree**—a tree that stays green all year

(continued on next page)

More words you need to know when you talk to trees:

 **Simple leaf**—a leaf whose stalk is attached directly to a twig

 **Compound leaf**—a leaf made up of several leaflets (little leaves) on a stalk that is attached to a twig

 **Flowering tree**—a tree that makes pollen and seeds in flowers and fruits

 **Conifer**—a tree that makes pollen and seeds inside its cones

 **Catkin**—a tree flower that hangs down from a twig and looks like a caterpillar or a little cat's tail

 **Pollen**—a yellowish powder made by male cones or flowers; pollen travels from one plant to another to help make seeds

 **Pine pitch**—a sticky, thick liquid in the bark of a pine tree

Lichen—a part-fungus, part-alga growth on tree trunks, rocks, or the ground; lichens do not hurt trees

You can learn about other kinds of trees in your neighborhood by checking out a tree identification book at your local library.

Some questions you can ask when you talk to trees:

 Does the tree have leaves or needles?

leaves   **needles**

■ If the tree has leaves,
are the leaves simple or compound?

simple leaf   **compound leaf**

■ If the tree has needles, are they
attached to the branch singly or in bundles?

single needles   **bundled needles**

■ If the tree has leaves, do they grow
opposite each other on the twig or
alternately?

opposite leaves   **alternate leaves**

■ Are the needles long or short?

■ Are the needles soft, or sharp
and prickly?

 Does the tree have flowers? What do they look like?

single   **cluster**   **cluster in petal-like bracts**   **catkins**

 Does the tree have fruit? What does it look like?
Look on the ground. You may find old fruit from last year.

nut   **berry**   **pod**   **cone**   **key**

Can you find any of these trees in your neighborhood?

Dogwood

 Simple leaf

 Tiny flowers in petal-like bracts

 Berries

Redbud

 Simple leaf

 Small, pink flowers

 Pods

Hickory

 Compound leaf

 Catkins

 Nuts

Blue spruce

 Single needles attached to twig

Cone

Sassafras

 Simple leaf

Cluster of small flowers

Berries

White oak

Simple leaf

Catkins

Acorns

Tulip tree

 Simple leaf

Large, tulip-shaped flower

Cone-like fruit

White pine

 Bundles of five needles

Cone

Red maple

 Simple leaf

Cluster of small flowers

Key

Walnut

 Compound leaf

Catkins

Nuts

Persimmon

 Simple leaf

Single, bell-shaped flowers

Large orange fruit